EUROPE

Rome

RUSSIA

Jerusalem

EGYPT

CHINA

Himalayas

Delhi

INDIA

AFRICA

·Great Barrier Reef

AUSTRALIA

ANTARCTICA

For all who love travel, in body or in mind – JR

To my two grandmothers, Eva Sugrue and Nora Huane – CC

Text copyright © Juliet Rix 2018
Illustrations copyright © Christopher Corr 2018

First published in Great Britain in 2018 and in the USA in 2019 by
Otter-Barry Books, Little Orchard, Burley Gate, Herefordshire, HR1 3QS
www.otterbarrybooks.com

A catalogue record for this book is available from the British Library.

ISBN 978-1-91095-934-3

Illustrated with gouache

Set in Mr Dodo

Printed in China

1 3 5 7 9 8 6 4 2

TRAVELS WITH MY GRANNY

Words by Juliet Rix

Pictures by Christopher Corr

Otter-Barry BOOKS

My Granny is a great traveller.
When she was younger she travelled all over the world.

To China...

Russia...

Egypt...

and Peru.

She crossed rivers and mountain ranges,
explored jungles and towering cities.

Now her legs won't carry her much further than the door, but she still travels...

and sometimes she takes me with her.

"Where are we, Granny?"
"We're in Delhi, silly."
"What's in Delhi, Granny?"
And she tells me all about it...

"Delhi is the capital of India."

"Hindu god Ganesha has the head of an elephant."

"Tricycle taxis called rickshaws roam the streets."

"Cricket is the most popular sport in India."

We've been to Rome...

Throw a coin over your shoulder
into the Trevi Fountain and you're
sure to return to Rome, (so they say)."

"Ancient Romans came to the Coliseum to watch gladiators fight."

"Italy is the home of ice cream and spaghetti."

S·P·Q·R CAESAR

"Mopeds are a popular way of travelling around Rome."

and Jerusalem...

"This city is 3,000 years old!"

"Jerusalem is sacred to Jews, Christians and Muslims.

"The tiny alleyways of Old Jerusalem are like a maze."

We've been to London...

"18 kings and queens are buried in Westminster Abbey."

"They're changing the guard at Buckingham Palace."

"They used to keep lions and tigers at the Tower of London."

"There are 33 bridges over the river Thames in London."

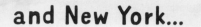

and New York...

"New York was the first city to have lots of skyscrapers."

"New York City taxis are yellow."

"The streets in the centre of the city are all in straight lines."

"Times Square is full of bright flashing lights – day and night."

The grown-ups say Granny is confused
and doesn't know where she is.

But I think she knows exactly where she is. It just isn't where the grown-ups are.

We've sailed the Great Lakes...

and hiked the Himalayas.

We've snorkelled the Great Barrier Reef...

and dined up the Eiffel Tower.

Sometimes Granny gets ahead
and I don't know where she's gone.

Then I have to wait until she returns...
and we set off again.

Granny can't remember yesterday,
but she knows all about the world.

That's fine with me. I can remember yesterday myself.
But I need my granny to take me travelling.

Where are we going next, Granny?

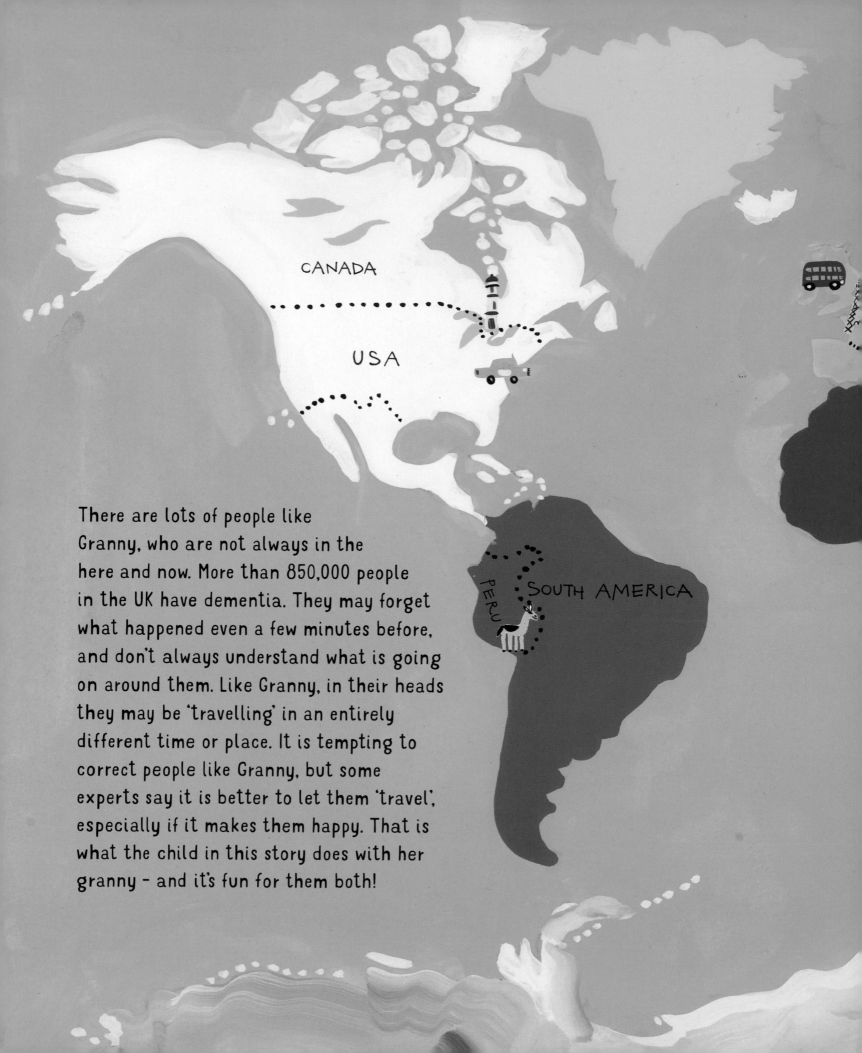

There are lots of people like Granny, who are not always in the here and now. More than 850,000 people in the UK have dementia. They may forget what happened even a few minutes before, and don't always understand what is going on around them. Like Granny, in their heads they may be 'travelling' in an entirely different time or place. It is tempting to correct people like Granny, but some experts say it is better to let them 'travel', especially if it makes them happy. That is what the child in this story does with her granny - and it's fun for them both!

CANADA

USA

PERU   SOUTH AMERICA